SYMBOL ART

upper left, Leo; *upper right,* Fixed Star; *lower left,* Sum; *lower right,* Hurricane

SYMBOL ART

Thirteen □s ○s △s from around the world

WRITTEN AND ILLUSTRATED BY
LEONARD EVERETT FISHER

FOUR WINDS PRESS
Macmillan Publishing Company New York

SPECIAL ACKNOWLEDGMENTS

I should like to thank the following organizations for permitting me to use their identifying symbols.

Aluminum Company of America, Pittsburgh, Pennsylvania
American Can Company, Greenwich, Connecticut
American Telephone and Telegraph Company, New York, New York
Chrysler Corporation, Detroit, Michigan
Chubb & Son, Incorporated, Short Hills, New Jersey
Irish Tourist Board, New York, New York
Motorola Incorporated, Schaumburg, Illinois
Rockwell International Corporation, Pittsburgh, Pennsylvania
Rohm and Haas Company, Philadelphia, Pennsylvania
The Maytag Company, Newton, Iowa
W. J. Barney Corporation, New York, New York
Weyerhauser Company, Tacoma, Washington

And special thanks to my wife, Margery, whose lively mind and librarianship seeded this book and its predecessors, ALPHABET ART and NUMBER ART.

Macmillan Publishing Company
866 Third Avenue, New York, N.Y. 10022
Collier Macmillan Canada, Inc.

Printed in the United States of America

10 9 8 7 6 5 4 3 2 1

The text of this book is set in 12 pt. Trump.
The illustrations are rendered in pen-and-ink and scratchboard.

Library of Congress Cataloging in Publication Data
Fisher, Leonard Everett.
Symbol art.
On t.p. "[square]" appears as the figure of a square;
"[circle]" appears as the figure of a circle;
"[triangle]" appears as the figure of a triangle.
Summary: Examines the use of symbols throughout the world and how they are used to communicate without words.
1. Signs and symbols—Juvenile literature.
[1. Signs and symbols] I. Title.
GR931.F57 1985 001.56 85-42805
ISBN 0-02-735270-6

SYMBOL ART

To communicate ideas unique to their special interests, various ancient and modern disciplines have used the simple square, circle and triangle.

SYSTEM	Square	Circle	Triangle
Astrology	Quadrate (90°)		Trigon (120°)
Astronomy	Quadrature (90°)	Full Moon	Trine (120°)
Biology and Botany	Male	Female	Evergreen
Chemistry (ancient)		Alum	
Engineering	1. Structural 2. Electrical Connection		
Language		1. Greek Omicron 2. Roman O 3. Cyrillic O 4. Gaelic O	1. Greek Delta 2. Eskimo A, I, U and AI
Mapmaking (not standard)	1. Building 2. Point of Interest	1. Town 2. City 3. Highway Interchange 4. Degree	1. Rest Area 2. Point of Interest
Mathematics	Square	1. Circle 2. Degree 3. No Value 4. 360°	1. Triangle 2. Increase
Medicine	Male	Female	
Printing	Em Measure		
Religion	Worldliness	1. Immortality 2. Eternity 3. Fire	1. Trinity 2. Immortality 3. Fire 4. Water
Weather	Tornado	1. Cloudless 2. Overcast	Showers

THE □ ○ △ OF SYMBOLS

A symbol is an image, sign or mark that stands for something else. The symbol can be an alphabetic letter signifying sound; a punctuation mark indicating emphasis, interruption or definition in writing and printing; a number standing for an amount; a *logo,* or design representing a business. In short, a symbol is any device created to communicate on sight the idea of a country, an event, an occupation, a business, a service, an idea itself and much more.

A flag can be a symbol for a school, a state, a nation or an award, among others. Even parts of the flag's design can represent ideas. The American flag, for example, is a rectangle composed of fifty stars, thirteen stripes and three colors—red, white and blue. The thirteen stripes stand for the original thirteen colonies. The fifty stars represent the fifty states. The red in the flag signifies courage and the blood that was shed for independence. The white symbolizes the purity and goodness of freedom and liberty. The blue represents the heavens against which are seen the white stars of the states, which altogether stand for a new constellation in the sky above: the United States of America. When the *Stars and Stripes* is flown, it immediately becomes a symbol identifying and characterizing the American presence.

Similarly, a pair of scissors or a needle and thread on a sign above a shop door immediately tell people what goes on inside, before anyone can read the word *tailor.* A line drawing of a gasoline pump on a highway sign quickly tells a motorist that a gasoline station is ahead. Symbols abound throughout the ancient and modern world in religion, government, the military, colleges and universities, science, mapmaking, travel, clubs, tribes, clans and countless other areas of life. Symbols then and now provide instant recognition of ideas, activities and organizations. This they do either by embodying something of what these things mean in a unit of design or by creating a design to identify them. Symbols cut across language barriers. They transcend grammar and vocabulary. They need no grammatical structure to be understood. A Peruvian shepherd and a Chinese farmer may not understand *veleno,* the Italian word for poison, when handling a bottle of chemicals manufactured in Italy. But both would quickly understand the peril inside the bottle if the label included an image of a skull and crossbones. That symbol indicates *poison, danger, death* in a universal language.

There are many more sets of symbols, ancient and modern, than appear in this book. Nevertheless, those included will introduce you to the ingenuity of people in inventing symbols and to the great variety of symbolic designs just in the thirteen areas of human thought and activity presented on the following pages.

WHEN SYMBOLS BEGAN

The appearance of symbols began with the prehistoric presence of human beings on earth in some dim moment of time, long before writing was invented to make spoken language visible. Some ten to fifteen thousand years ago prehistoric people in Central Europe and elsewhere carved and painted various figures, animals and objects on the walls of their caves. Roaring bisons, placid mammoths, pregnant tigers, wounded reindeer, dancing humans, the sun and the moon—the exact meaning of these carvings and paintings is unknown. Nevertheless, it is reasonable to assume that these early artists were not simply indulging themselves in self-expression. The deep, dark caves in which the early hunters carved and painted their images were more likely sacred places, the sites of magical ceremonies. Here early people symbolized their rituals of worship with representations of life as they knew it.

THE LOOK OF SYMBOLS

A group of logos designed to identify various businesses appears on pages 30 and 31. The square, the circle and the triangle are the basic shapes for all these logos. Even the astrological symbols on pages 14 and 15 involve the use of these three basic shapes in arriving at the intricacy of their designs.

Whatever the symbol, however plain or complex, however unusual its appearance—its design is based on the general geometry of the square, circle or triangle; or variations and combinations of the square, circle and triangle; or parts of the square, circle and triangle. A complicated flag design can be created within a rectangular or square banner or a triangular pennant. The fireball sun can be symbolized by a simple circle, as can the human head on a stick figure, a "no value" zero in a mathematical computation and the letter *O* in the Roman alphabet. A simple square can symbolize a printing measure, a historic site on a map or a male figure in biological notation. In fact, the square, circle and triangle are the basic shapes from which all drawn, painted and printed images, or *graphic design,* derive.

top to bottom: Mathematics, Religion, Weather, Astronomy

THE SYMBOLS

ASTROLOGY

ASTRONOMY

BIOLOGY / BOTANY

BUSINESS

BUSINESS LOGO

CHEMISTRY

MAGIC

MATHEMATICS

MUSIC

PRINTING

RELIGION

SHORTHAND

WEATHER

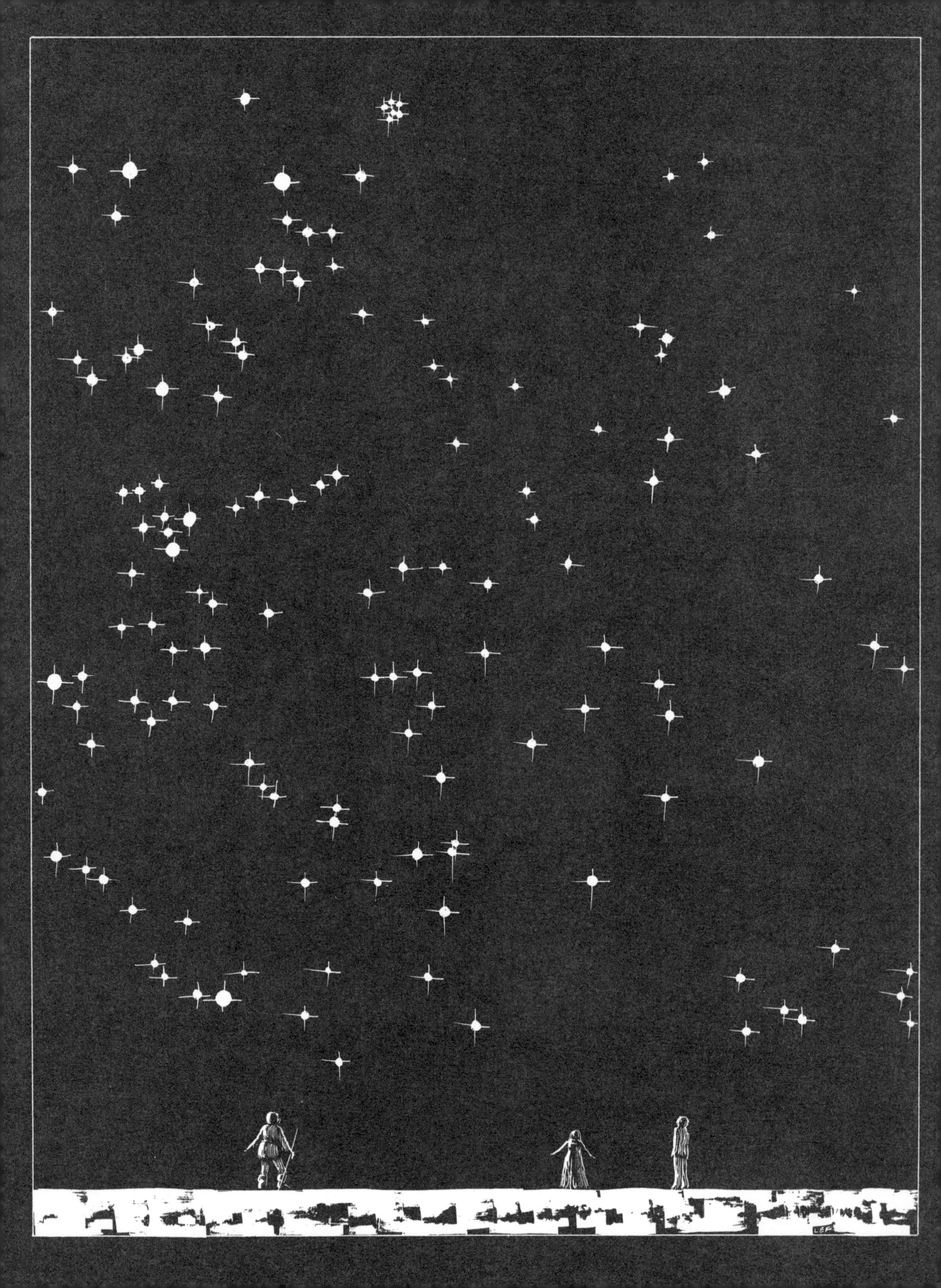

ASTROLOGY

The sky was a vast and overwhelming mystery to the farmers of ancient Babylonia. Unable to explain the physical nature of the sun, moon and stars, the Babylonians believed these heavenly bodies to be gods. The five planets known to us by the Roman names of Mercury, Venus, Mars, Saturn and Jupiter were thought to be gods as well. Moreover, all the stars had special significance, either individually or in groups called *constellations.* The Babylonians and those who followed—chiefly Egyptians, Greeks and Romans—did not look for explanations: As far as they were concerned, gods did not owe mere humans explanations. It was enough that their movements, their comings and goings overhead, influenced every event on earth, from one's personal welfare and the success of the crops to the survival of kingdoms. It was crucial to observe the movements of the sun, moon, planets and stars to read the "signs." If one could read the signs properly, one could predict the future. Fortune-telling was the essence of astrology in the ancient world and, to a large extent, remains the essence of astrology today.

Complicated charts, or *horoscopes,* were devised to read the signs and predict the future. Their computations were based on the idea that the earth stood still at the center of the universe; that an invisible zone called a *zodiac* ran around the earth; and that the sun, moon, planets and stars traveled through this zone. The zodiac was divided into twelve parts, or *houses.* Each house had an individual *sign* to identify it and characterize its special qualities and functions.

The signs on the following pages are a blend of Babylonian, Greek and Roman graphic imagery first devised nearly three thousand years ago, further developed over the following one thousand years, modified and refined into the modern era.

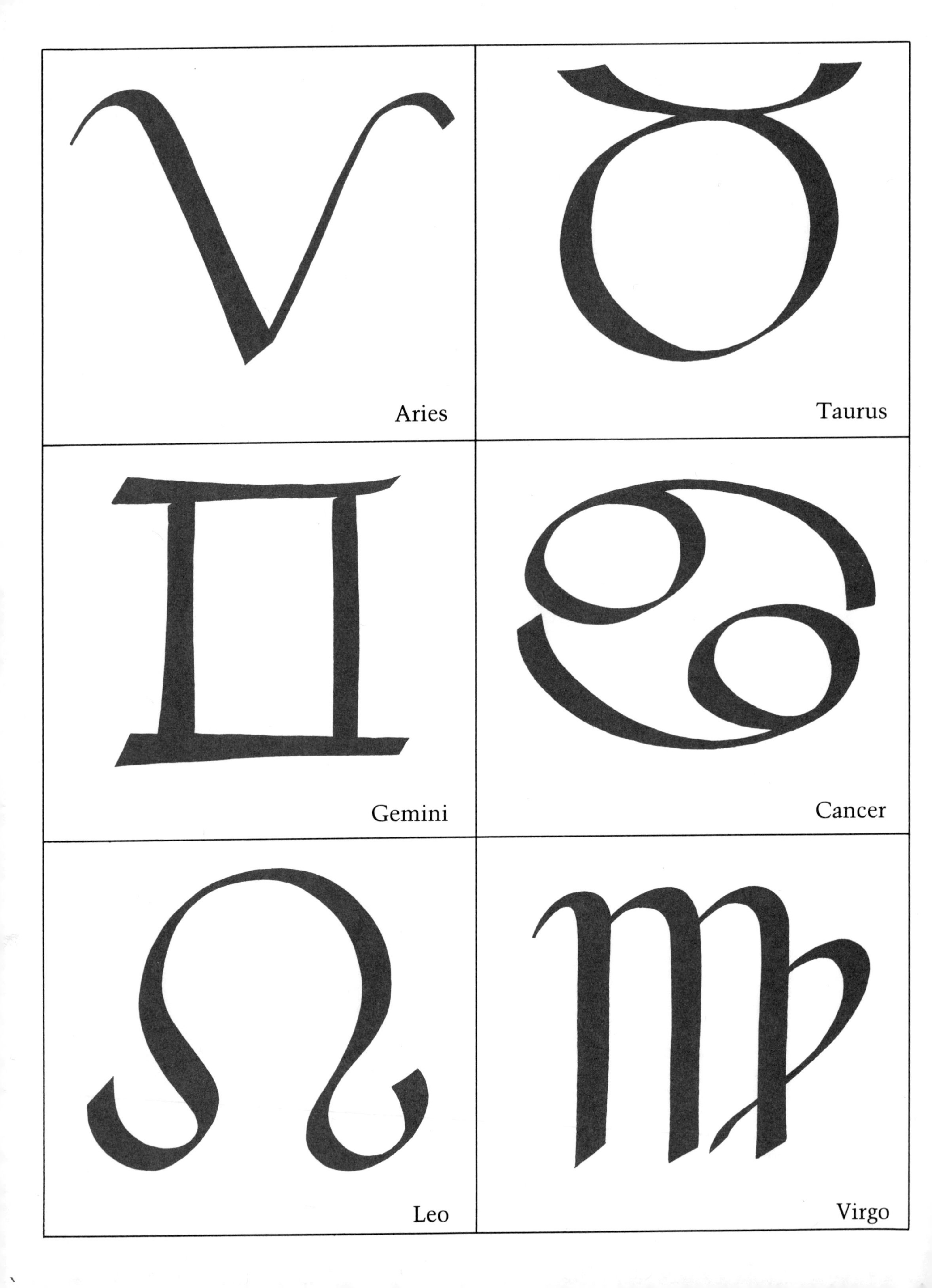
Aries
Taurus
Gemini
Cancer
Leo
Virgo

Libra
Scorpio
Sagittarius
Capricorn
Aquarius
Pisces

LEF

ASTRONOMY

From the unrecorded past to this day, people have measured their earthly existence by the movements of heavenly bodies. They have sought to explain their own nature and predict their own future by calculating the rhythms of the sun, moon, planets and stars. They have seen good and evil in these movements and used sky-based calculations to deal with human affairs. This study of heavenly motion as it affects human behavior—*astrology* (see pages 12–15)—began to lose popularity during the 1500s, toward the end of the Renaissance in Europe.

In 1543, Polish-born Nicolaus Copernicus, an astronomer, offered a theory that established *astronomy*—the study of laws governing the physical nature of heavenly bodies—as an exact science. A few ancient astronomers had long suspected what Copernicus finally argued: that the earth was not motionless at the center of the universe; that the earth, its moon, the known planets and their moons traveled around the sun; that the zodiac did not exist. Copernicus's treatise *Concerning the Revolutions of the Celestial Spheres* came at a time when people were questioning the unexplainable. They wanted answers based on facts, not magic and guesswork. New waves of thinking demanded truth founded on facts. Although the struggle between old and new—between astrology and astronomy—raged on for many years, the advent of astronomy heralded the arrival of the modern era. Today, astronomy's mixture of old and new symbols of notation is a reminder of its link to the past.

The Sun
The Moon
New Moon
First Quarter Moon
Full Moon
Last Quarter Moon
A Fixed Star
Mercury
Venus
Earth
Mars
Jupiter

Saturn
Uranus
Neptune
Pluto
A Comet
Conjunction
Sextile
60 degrees distance
Quadrature
90 degrees distance
Trine or Distance
120 degrees distance
Opposition
Ascending Node
Descending Node

BIOLOGY / BOTANY

Biology is the study of all living organisms. There are two main branches of biology: *zoology,* the study of animal life, and *botany,* the study of plant life. Several biological sciences cut across both zoology and botany: *pathology, cytology, taxonomy, morphology* and *ecology*—the studies of diseases, cells, classifications, structures and environments, respectively.

Botany is one of the oldest sciences. The first nomadic hunters and cave dwellers gained wide knowledge of plant life for practical reasons. Plants were a food source, and early humans had to be able to tell the difference between edible plants and poisonous ones. The value of many plants as medicine was also gradually discovered. Plants such as trees provided material for crude constructions, while other reed-like plants could be woven into clothing.

But the modern science of botany had its awakening in Renaissance Europe (*c.* 1300–1500). Scholars then began to realize that better information about plants was needed. Plants raised as crops had become the chief world food supply. The botanical writings of the ancient Hebrews, Egyptians, Greeks, Romans and others were inadequate, confusing or wrong. It was not until the mid-1600s that anyone knew how plants grew from seeds. About one hundred fifty years later, Carl Linnaeus, a Swedish botanist, classified plants as male or female and developed a system that facilitated the study of plant life. More recently, powerful electronic equipment has made possible intense studies in plant *genetics,* or hereditary characteristics, and cell structure—studies that can affect the well-being of the entire human population.

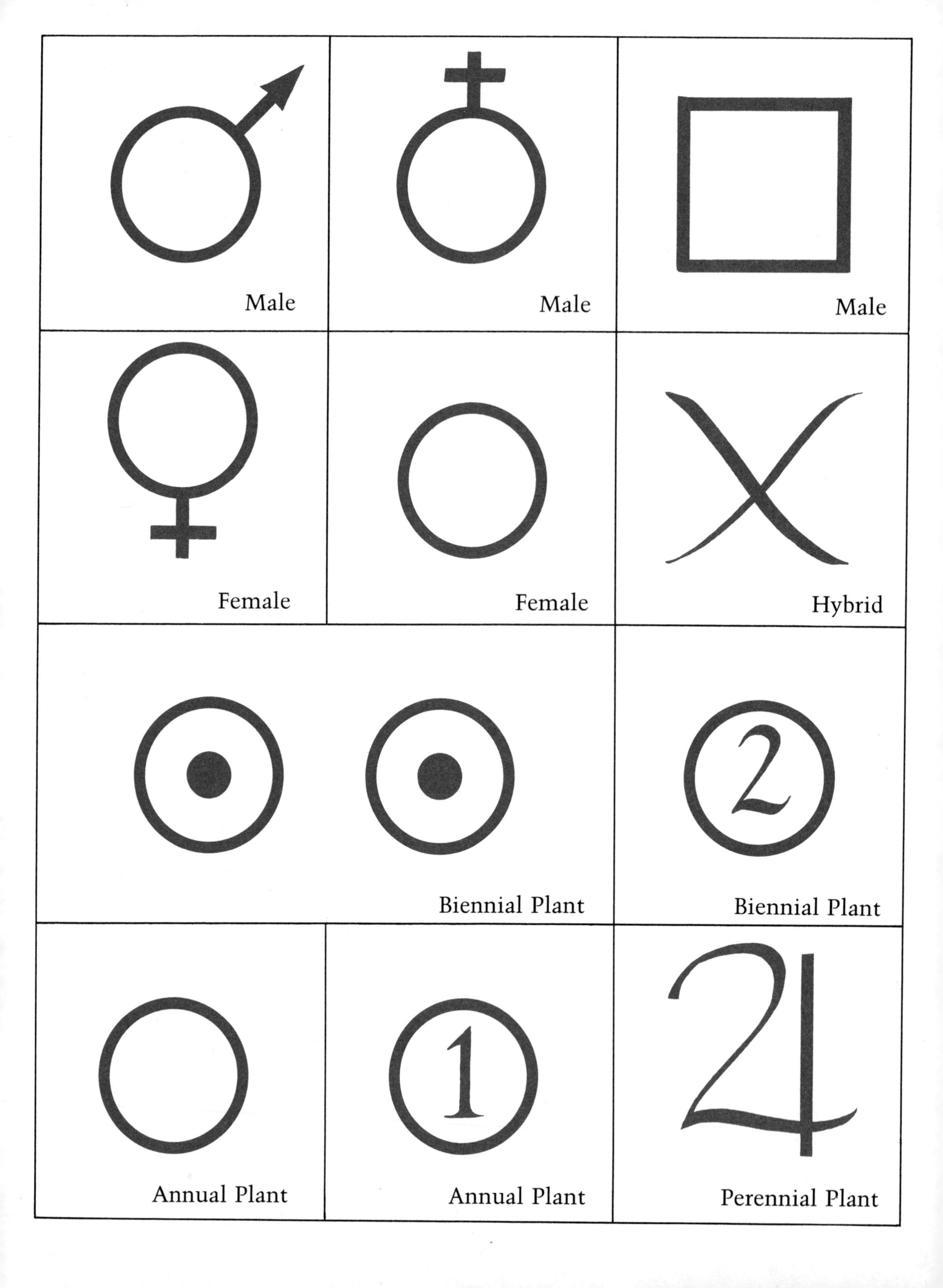
Male
Male
Male
Female
Female
Hybrid
Biennial Plant
Biennial Plant
Annual Plant
Annual Plant
Perennial Plant

Indefinite
Climber
Perfect Plant
Northern Hemisphere
Southern Hemisphere
Bears Fruit Only Once
Eastern Hemisphere
Western Hemisphere
Evergreen
Tree or Shrub
Tree
Shrub

BUSINESS

Five thousand years ago, Phoenician merchants sent their ships around the Mediterranean Sea and their caravans overland to the land of biblical Abraham in the Tigris-Euphrates Valley of Mesopotamia. They did a good business selling their fruit, produce, textiles, wares and weapons. Western civilization was in its infancy. The first of Egypt's five great epochs had not yet begun.

Much of the trade then consisted of *barter*—the exchange of goods of equal value. Equal value was determined by the traders themselves as they haggled their way to what each trader thought was a bargain. Between tribes or nations, there was no exchange of currency for goods. Any organized group of people that *had* its own hard currency would not think of exchanging it for foreign currency. Any money exchanges occurred within the group.

These wily Phoenician traders developed a written language, chiefly to record their business transactions. They kept records of what they bought and sold by devising an alphabet from other already-written Semitic tongues, contracting words and permitting letter symbols to communicate their hurried meaning, creating perhaps the earliest business symbols. The Phoenician word for "goods," for example, might have been abbreviated into "gds." or "barrels" to "bls."

Symbols like the more-modern dollar sign *$* have developed from similar abbreviations and contractions. Perhaps the dollar sign was derived from the initials *U.S.*, meaning "United States." In this instance, a monogram was created by overlapping the two letters. Eventually, shortcut handwriting eliminated the bottom arc of the *U* and the dollar sign was born to indicate United States currency.

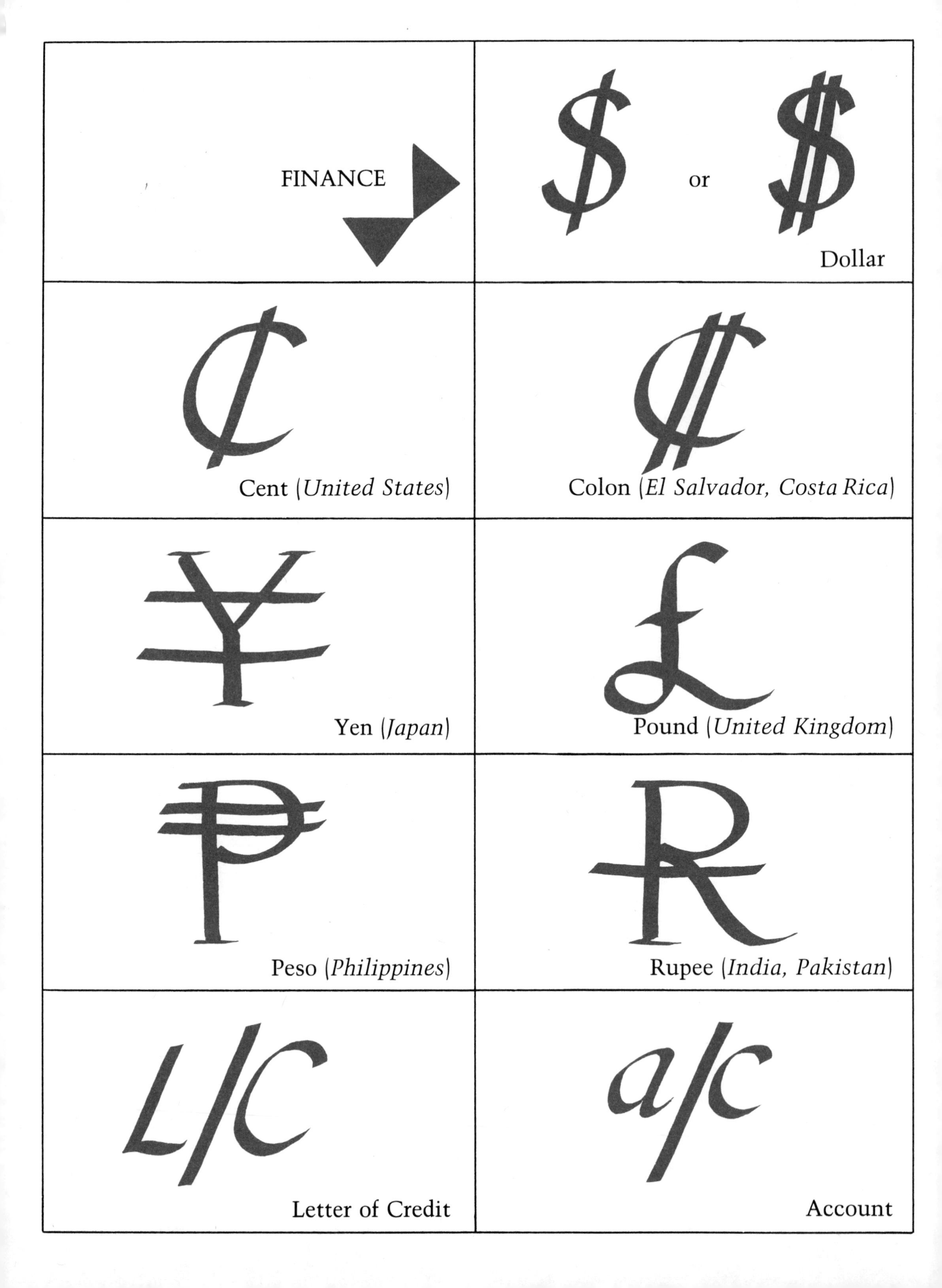

FINANCE
or
Dollar
Cent (*United States*)
Colon (*El Salvador, Costa Rica*)
Yen (*Japan*)
Pound (*United Kingdom*)
Peso (*Philippines*)
Rupee (*India, Pakistan*)
L/C
Letter of Credit
a/c
Account

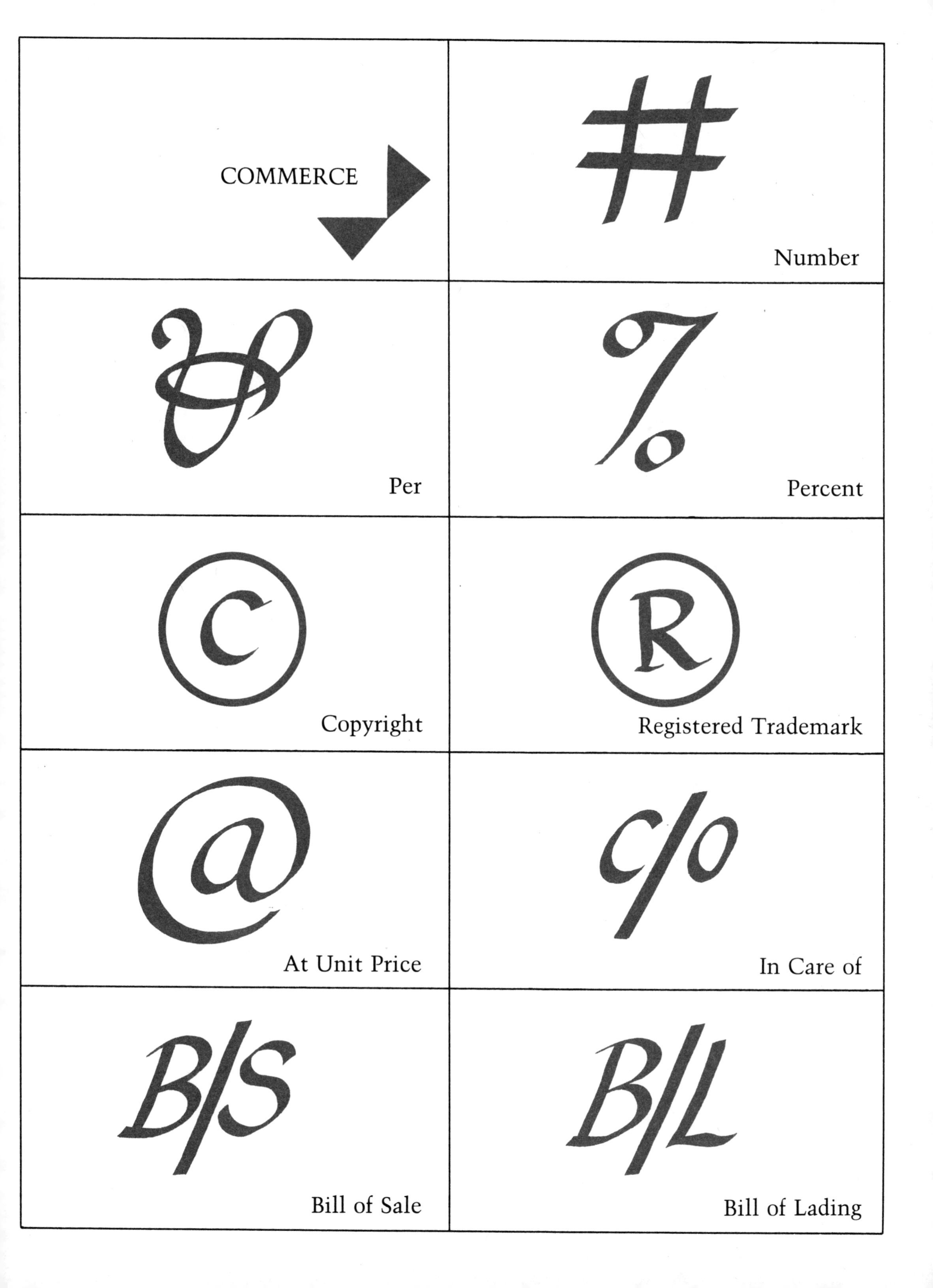
COMMERCE
Number
Per
Percent
Copyright
Registered Trademark
At Unit Price
In Care of
Bill of Sale
Bill of Lading

BUSINESS LOGO

Logo is a shortened version of *logotype.* A logotype is a graphic symbol instantly identifying a business, a company, an agency or a corporation. *Trademarks* and logos are quite similar. But trademarks have come to identify individual products, while logos more often suggest the broad image of a company. When Towle's Log Cabin Syrup became a marketable product in the 1880s, a log cabin—to honor Abraham Lincoln—was used on the can, symbolizing both the company and its product, maple syrup. The entire world soon knew what that log cabin stood for. When the General Foods Corporation purchased Towle's in 1929, the log cabin remained as the syrup's symbol, or trademark. It became one of the many trademarks related to a variety of products made by the General Foods Corporation. And the corporation symbolized itself with a logo representing the company as a whole and having no resemblance to any of its product trademarks. Similarly, book publishers use the *colophon,* an ornamental design on book covers or title pages, to represent the image of the company as a whole.

Long before today's graphic designers began to create logos, craftsmen, merchants and traders used symbols, or *marks,* to identify themselves and their guilds, to guarantee business contracts or the quality of their workmanship, and to signify their professional pride. From the beginning of the Middle Ages (*c.* A.D. 450) to the beginning of the Industrial Revolution (*c.* A.D. 1750), a span of some thirteen hundred years, painters, sculptors, weavers, goldsmiths, printers, shippers, merchants and others all developed unique identifying symbols, usually taking the form of ornamental initials, or *monograms,* of the master craftsmen and merchant princes themselves.

On the following pages are twelve logos representing the pride, quality and goodwill of twentieth-century companies.

The Maytag Company
Chubb & Son, Incorporated
Motorola Incorporated
American Telephone and
Telegraph Company
Chrysler Corporation
Weyerhauser Company

Aluminum Company of America

Rohm and Haas Company

Irish Tourist Board

Rockwell International Corporation

American Can Company

W. J. Barney Corporation

Lead
Gold
LEF

CHEMISTRY

Chemistry is the *science,* or knowledge gained by systematic study, of the structure and properties of substances and the changes they undergo to become other substances having different structures and properties. Acrylic resin, for example, is a plastic substance having properties unlike those of the crude oil, coal, water and air compounds used to produce it.

Chemistry is a recent science, although ancient ironworkers used "chemistry" to produce hard metal from ore and people of every ancient civilization produced medicines from a variety of natural substances. The words *chemistry* and *chemical* have two related classical Greek roots: *chemi,* meaning black; and *chemeia,* meaning the process of changing lead into gold. Changing lead into gold—a process called alchemy—was the chief "chemical" preoccupation of the ancient Greeks, Romans and earlier people. All they succeeded in doing was making the grayish metal black, a far cry from the glittering gold they wanted. Yet, the idea that lead could become gold persisted into the Middle Ages. But medieval alchemists were so frustrated in their attempts that they resorted to secret rites and magic prayers—usually calling on the Devil himself—to give them, not only lead-induced gold, but also the secret to everlasting life. None of these practices received the blessing of the medieval church, which referred to alchemy as a "black art"; nor were the practices considered legal by rulers and parliaments, who feared that gold might come into hands other than their own. Operating as shadowy, mysterious figures, medieval alchemists developed a language of chemical symbols from which are derived most of the symbols used today in modern chemistry.

Alcohol
Alkali
Alum
Alum
Amalgam
Anglesite
Antimony
Arsenic
Bolus
Borax
Brimstone
Copiapate
Glass
Hematite
Iron
Lapis Lazuli

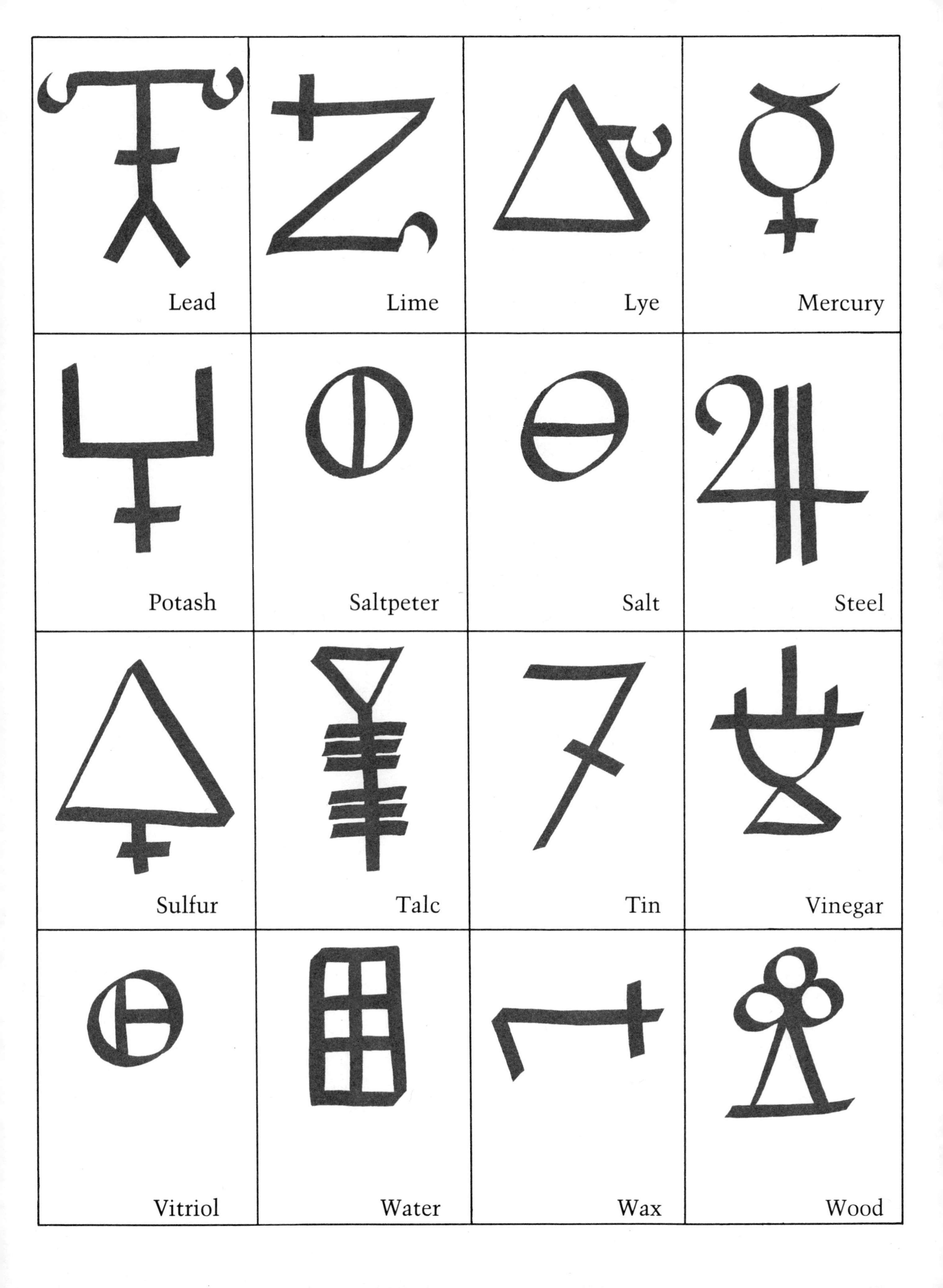
Lead
Lime
Lye
Mercury
Potash
Saltpeter
Salt
Steel
Sulfur
Talc
Tin
Vinegar
Vitriol
Water
Wax
Wood

LEF

MAGIC

Fear of the unknown and the unexplainable has governed human existence from the beginning to this day. Unable to explain a volcanic eruption or a tidal wave, for example, early people—and even the ancient Greeks and Romans—reasoned that a god had been offended and was showing anger. Every degree of good and evil power has been assigned to various events, natural objects and imaginary spirits. Supernatural beings have fascinated the human mind.

A child of ignorance, fear drove people in many societies, both primitive and modern, to seek mysterious magic defenses. People have created magic devices, writings and symbols to protect themselves against imaginary beings and against actual happenings beyond their understanding. How does day become night and then day again? Who, what and why was the sun? A comet? Earthquakes, famines, floods, fires, thunder, lightning, birth, life, sickness, death, the changing seasons all required special consideration to deal with their mysteries. *Amulets,* or charms of various designs often worn around the neck, were thought to have magic power to protect the wearer from harm. Some people still wear them!

Magicians became important in the affairs of early communities and civilizations. They convinced everyone of their mysterious power to ward off trouble. They drew mystical symbols, recited special words, or *incantations,* and cast *spells* creating enchanted states. Those whose symbols, incantations and spells brought evil were thought to be witches and sorcerers who practiced "black magic." Medieval alchemists (see pages 32–35) sought magic solutions in their quest to create gold out of other minerals. Lovers drank "love potions" for romance. Others rubbed objects and symbols for health, wealth and long life.

Long Life *(Egyptian)*

Protection against Fire *(Chinese)*

Protection against Witchcraft
(Scandinavian Rune)

Good Luck *(American Indian)*

Witch's Foot *(Celtic)*

Long Life *(Japanese)*

Magic Circle *(Islamic)*

Court for Witches *(German)*

LEF

MATHEMATICS

The study of the relationships between quantities, figures and forms is called *mathematics.* There are various branches of mathematics, such as arithmetic, algebra, geometry, trigonometry and calculus. The first cave dwellers did simple arithmetic when they added one scratch to another on the face of a rock to indicate the number of deer in a nearby herd or subtracted one stone from a group of stones to indicate a missing goat. As more organized communities developed, mathematical skills improved to satisfy more complex needs. Because they developed an understanding of basic geometry, ancient people like the Babylonians and Egyptians could survey land, measure distance and construct straight buildings essential to the progress of their civilizations.

From the time of the first city dwellers through Classical Greece—a period of about six thousand years—simple mathematical systems were developed using amount symbols, or *numbers,* and instructional symbols, like +, to make the job of computing less cumbersome, quicker and clearer. This practical, or *applied,* mathematics related to everyday problems of counting, keeping accounts, construction, commerce and conquest. The Greeks had additional needs, however. Greek philosophers used mathematics to solve problems dealing with space and volume and find solutions having no everyday practical application. This was *theoretical* mathematics. It set the stage for the later emergence of modern mathematics and the probing of our solar system and the universe beyond. It would have been impossible to widen our knowledge of time, space, form and motion without symbols developed over centuries of mathematical problem solving.

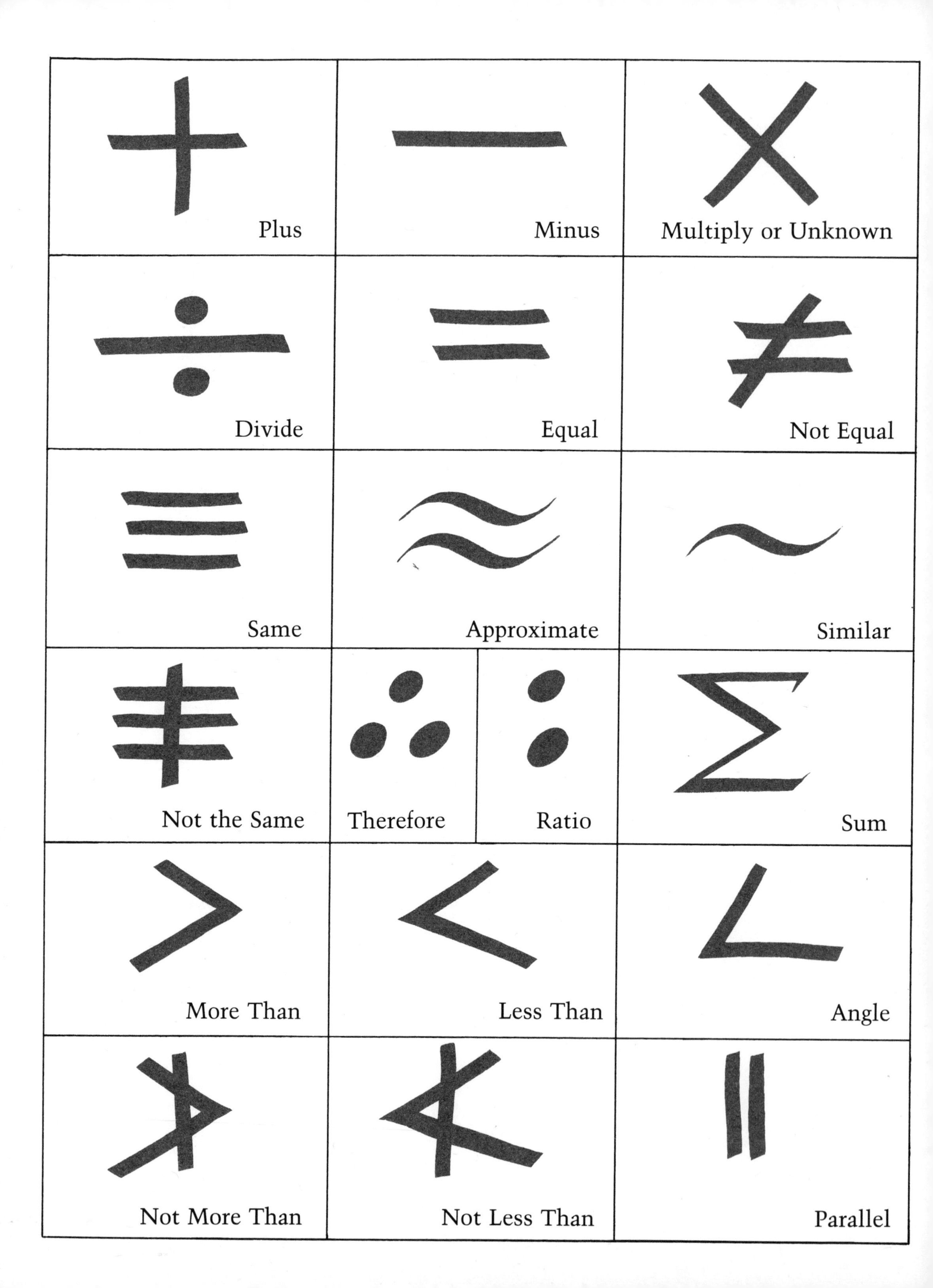

Plus
Minus
Multiply or Unknown
Divide
Equal
Not Equal
Same
Approximate
Similar
Not the Same
Therefore
Ratio
Sum
More Than
Less Than
Angle
Not More Than
Not Less Than
Parallel

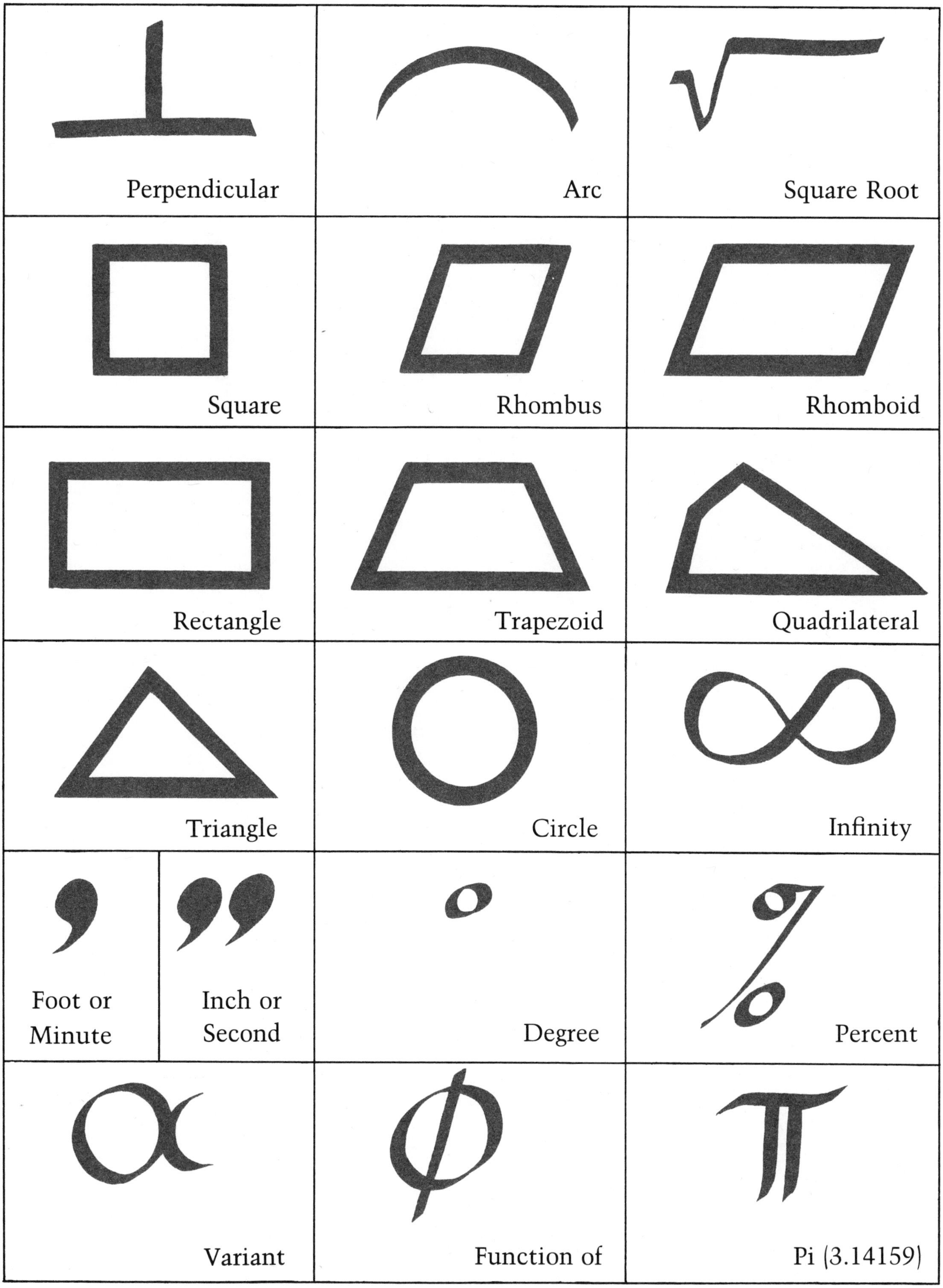

Perpendicular

Arc

Square Root

Square

Rhombus

Rhomboid

Rectangle

Trapezoid

Quadrilateral

Triangle

Circle

Infinity

Foot or Minute

Inch or Second

Degree

Percent

Variant

Function of

Pi (3.14159)

MUSIC

Rhythmical tones—*music*—have been in our lives ever since men, women and children first danced to the sound of clapping hands or the thud of a drum. Every community of people since the dawn of time has had its share of music and music makers.

Six thousand years ago, Egyptians and other people of the Middle East listened to the sounds of harps, drums, horns and cymbals. Farther east, Chinese and Indian music makers strummed zithers and played flutes. Much of the music created in these early epochs of developing civilizations had religious significance. Yet, no one thought of writing down the musical notes so that the sound of meaningful music could pass from one musician to another and from one generation to another. In fact, communicating anything by writing was not an achieved skill.

The Greeks were the first to symbolize musical sound. They were interested in accurate representation and performance of their music because of its role in their drama and dance. Using the letters of their alphabet, they developed a simple letter-notation method to write music for their theatrical choruses and various instruments.

In time, however, music became too complex for the Greek method. The Romans, for instance, invented new instruments, such as a pipe organ and a tuba, with new sounds the Greek notation system could not accommodate. By the Middle Ages, musical forms far too complicated to represent in the old notation were established, chiefly in the area of church music. By A.D. 1000, composers of church music were desperately seeking a symbol method to write music so that the music of the church could be played again and again in the same way. Guido d'Arezzo, an eleventh-century Italian Benedictine monk, provided the method: He invented the parallel lined scale, or *staff,* the notes and their names—*do, re, mi, fa, sol, la, ti*—that we use today to write music.

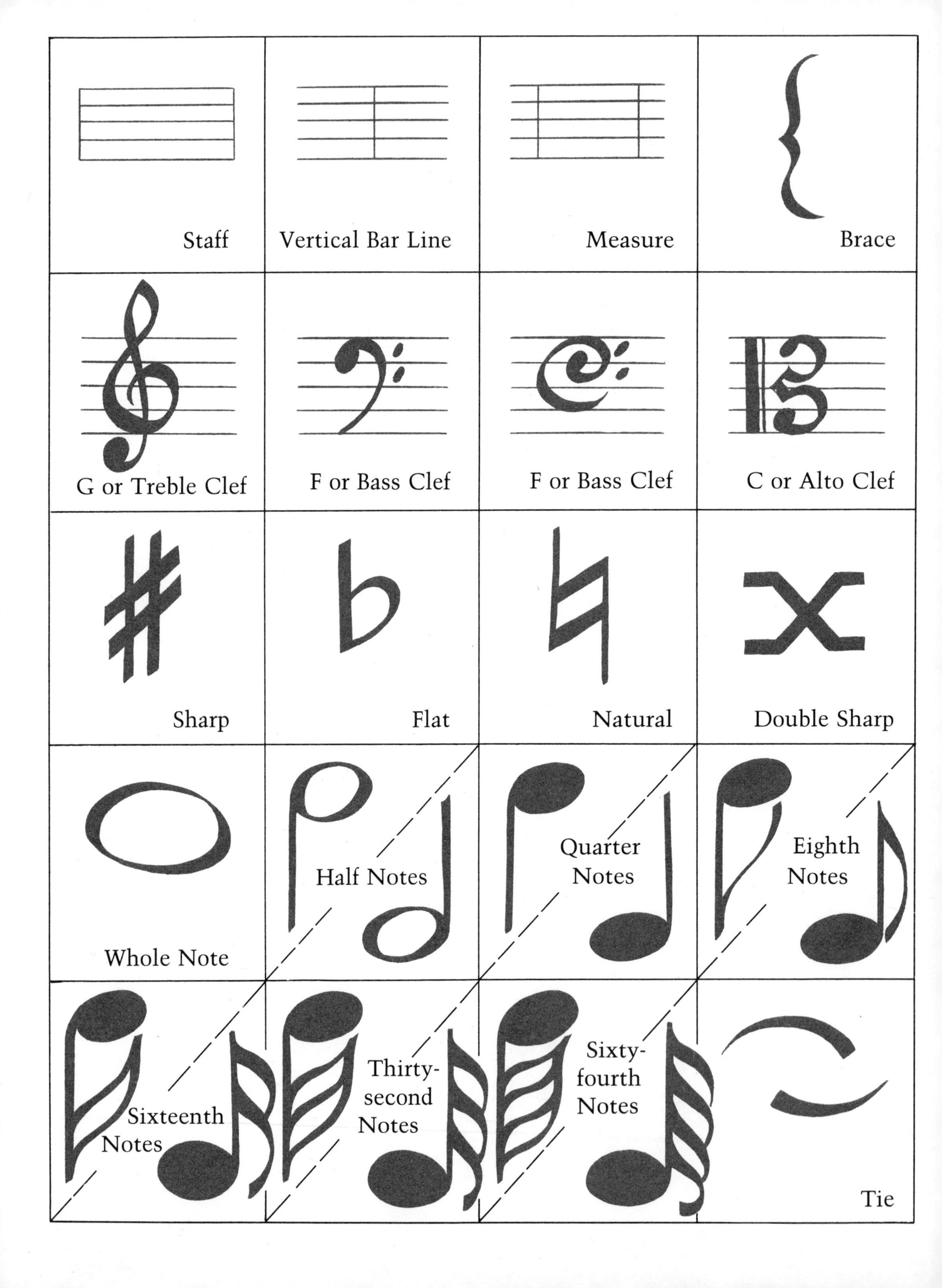
Staff
Vertical Bar Line
Measure
Brace
G or Treble Clef
F or Bass Clef
F or Bass Clef
C or Alto Clef
Sharp
Flat
Natural
Double Sharp
Whole Note
Half Notes
Quarter Notes
Eighth Notes
Sixteenth Notes
Thirty-second Notes
Sixty-fourth Notes
Tie

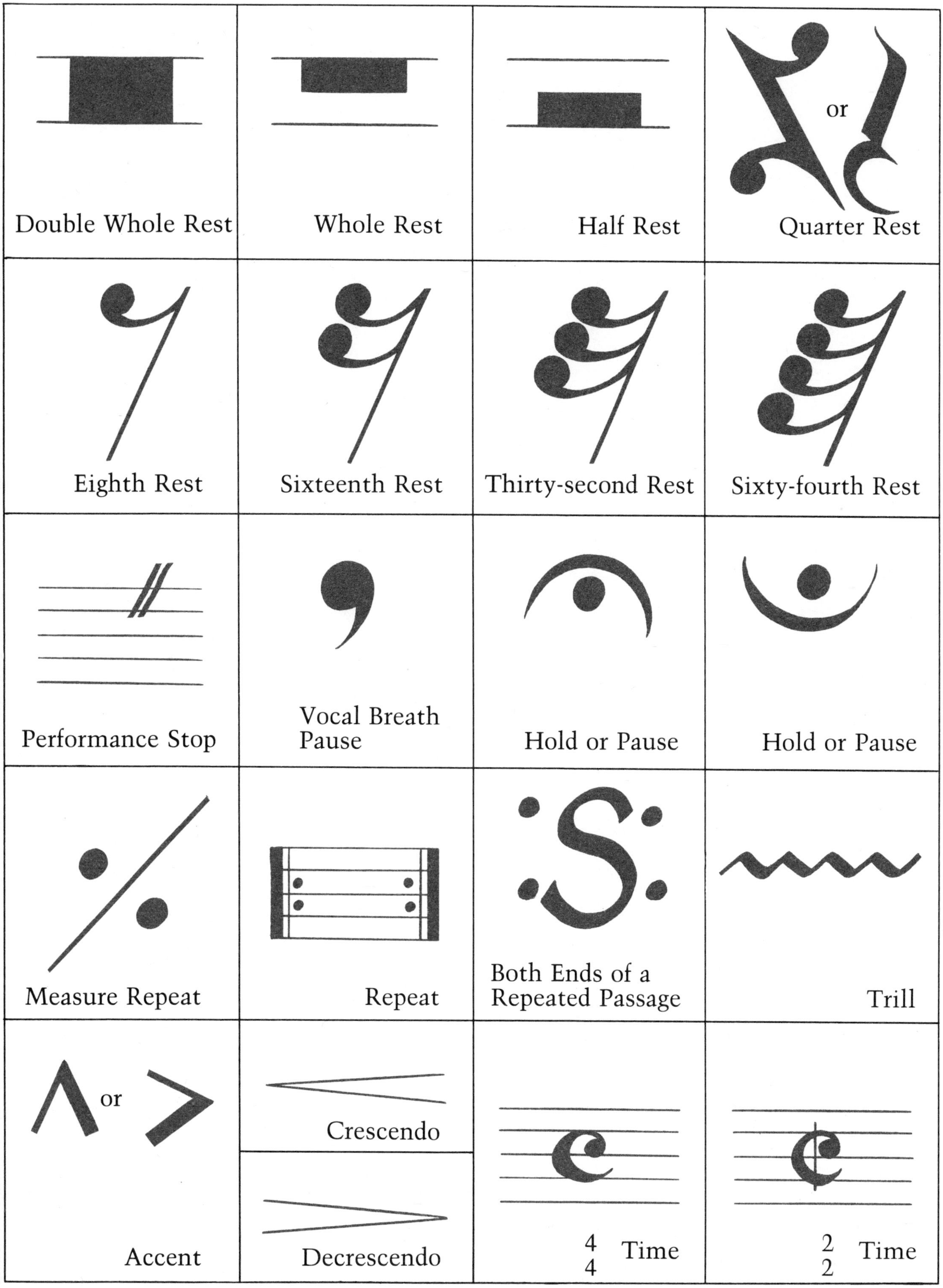

Double Whole Rest	Whole Rest	Half Rest	or Quarter Rest
Eighth Rest	Sixteenth Rest	Thirty-second Rest	Sixty-fourth Rest
Performance Stop	Vocal Breath Pause	Hold or Pause	Hold or Pause
Measure Repeat	Repeat	Both Ends of a Repeated Passage	Trill
or Accent	Crescendo Decrescendo	$\frac{4}{4}$ Time	$\frac{2}{2}$ Time

Johann Gutenberg
LEF

PRINTING

Between 1435 and 1445, German-born Johannes Gutenberg printed a Bible using movable, reusable metal type. He was the first European to move language from hand-lettered scrolls, manuscripts and books to the press-printed page. The Chinese had tried four hundred years earlier without success. Gutenberg and his fellow printers used paper and special inks invented by the Chinese more than a thousand years earlier, however.

Gutenberg's innovation immeasurably improved people's ability to communicate ideas and information in quantity, to a wide audience, fast, accurately and efficiently. Until Gutenberg, books and manuscripts were painstakingly written out by hand in very limited numbers. Few people could read. No standard way to spell a word, no precise rules of capitalization, punctuation or even grammar had been established. And, since each manuscript was one-of-a-kind, there were no test runs, or *proofs,* of each laboriously hand-lettered page to check for form, language and accuracy.

After Gutenberg's press, there was an overwhelming flood of printed matter. Since the movable type made possible proofs of every printed page, printers could now check over their proof sheets for accuracy before running off hundreds of copies on their presses. Various languages slowly took on common and acceptable forms so that the increasing numbers of readers would share the same conventions. Over the centuries, printers developed a system of symbols and abbreviations called "proofreader's marks" to call attention to those parts of each printed page that needed adjustment or correction.

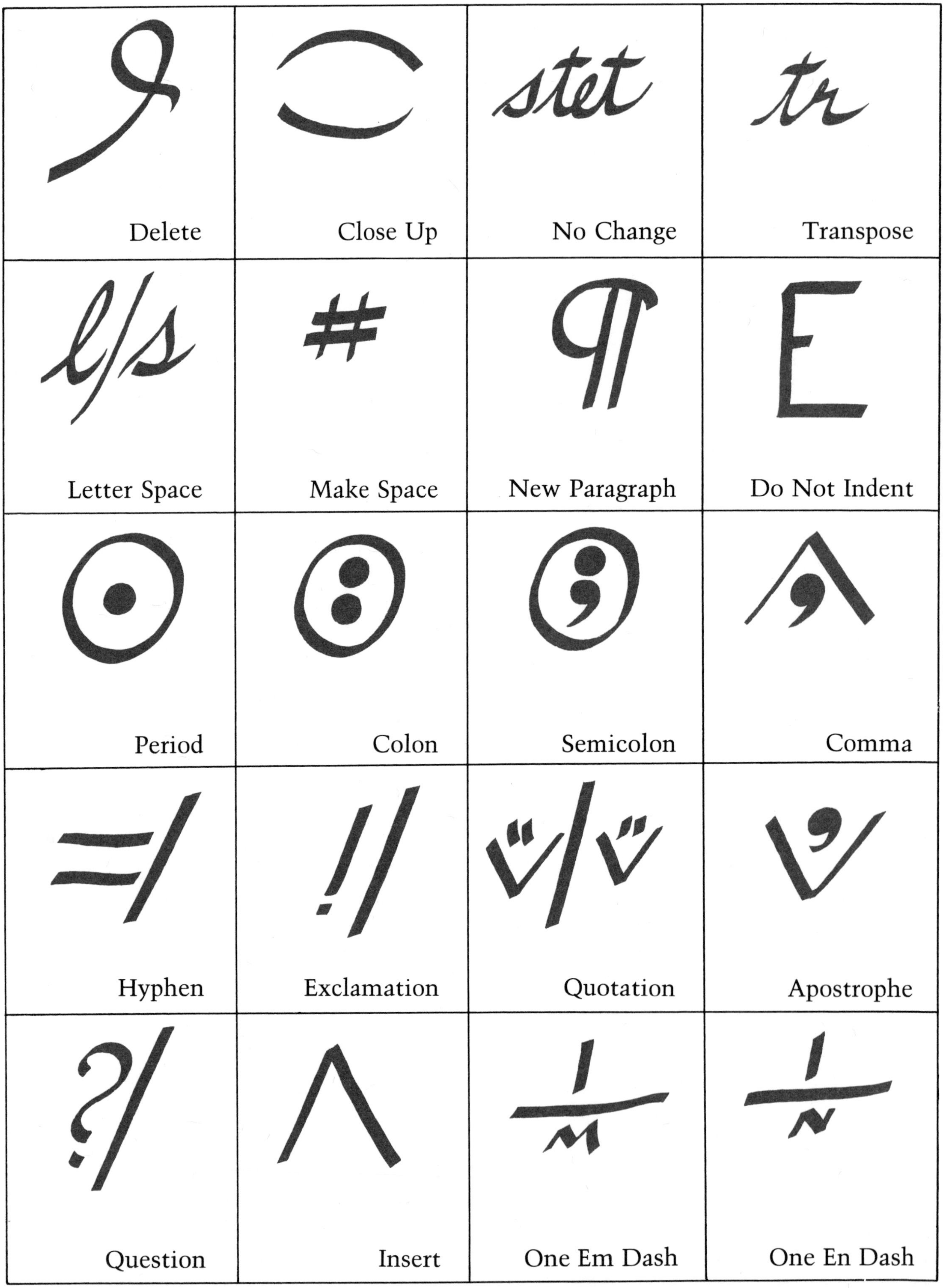

Delete	Close Up	stet No Change	tr Transpose
l/s Letter Space	# Make Space	¶ New Paragraph	Do Not Indent
Period	Colon	Semicolon	Comma
Hyphen	Exclamation	Quotation	Apostrophe
Question	Insert	One Em Dash	One En Dash

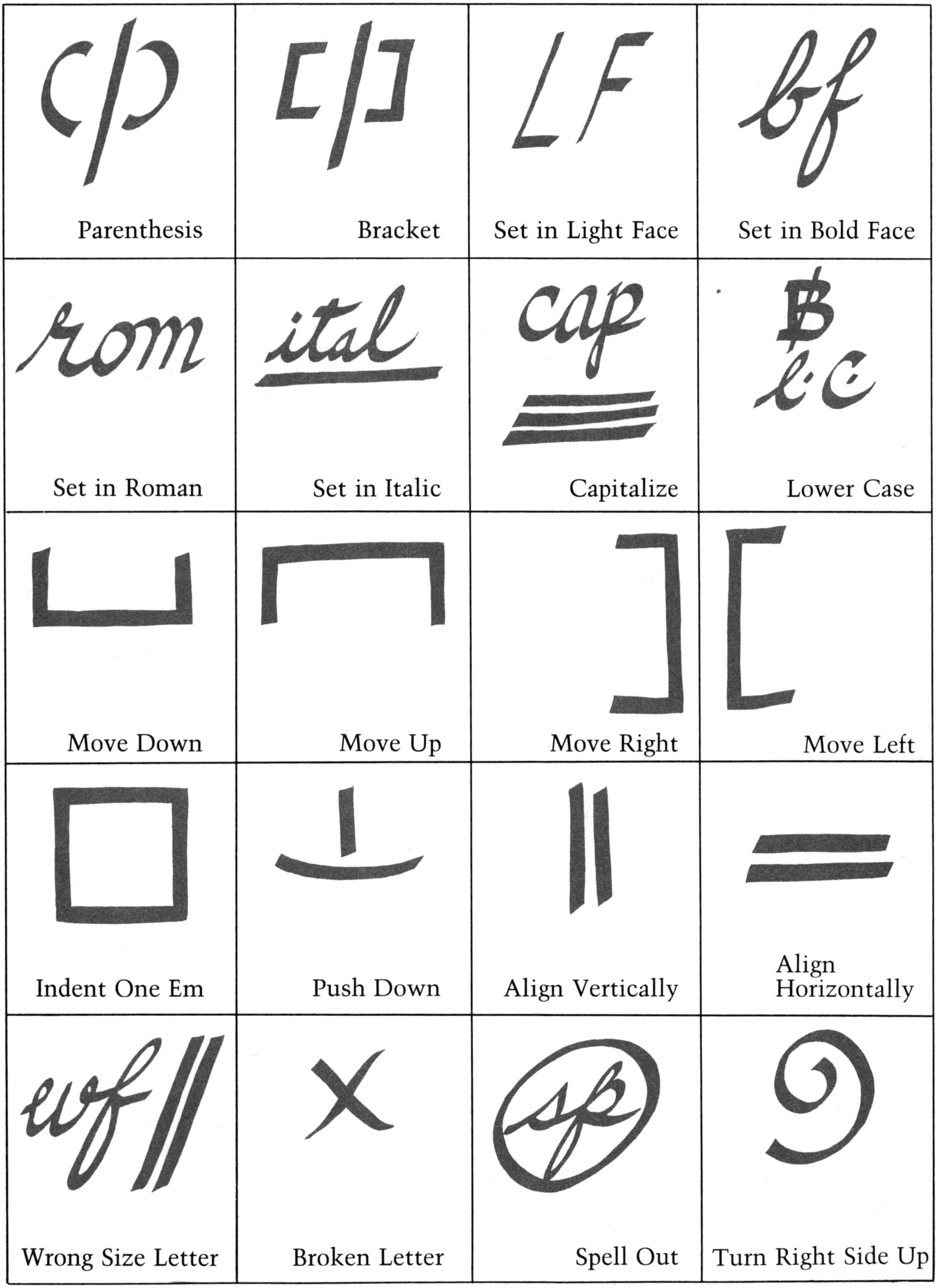
c/p
Parenthesis
[/]
Bracket
LF
Set in Light Face
bf
Set in Bold Face
rom
Set in Roman
ital
Set in Italic
cap
Capitalize
lc
Lower Case
Move Down
Move Up
Move Right
Move Left
Indent One Em
Push Down
Align Vertically
Align Horizontally
wf
Wrong Size Letter
Broken Letter
sp
Spell Out
Turn Right Side Up

RELIGION

When a group of people organizes activities around an abstract, eternal force greater than itself—a power called "God" or "Allah," for example—it is said to be *religious.* By asking for and receiving direction from God through its religious practices, any particular group, or *religion,* links the destinies of its members. Around the world there are a variety of religions and religious practices differing in appearances, rituals and rules, each religious group seeking to strengthen its connection with the divine in its own unique way.

The world's major religions—Christianity, Judaism, Islam, Hinduism, Buddhism and Shinto—did not appear suddenly. They emerged, following a long, difficult period of time, from primitive people's belief that all occurrences were the result of unseen living powers at work. There was no other way to explain the mysteries of light and dark, life and death, thunder and lightning, the sun and moon, floods and droughts, the course of rivers and the tides of the sea. These and many other manifestations of unseen powers became the basis of early beliefs in many gods and goddesses, or *polytheism.* With the emergence of Judaism, about 1200 B.C., as an influence in religious thought, polytheism began to give way among many people to *monotheism,* a belief in one God, a powerful being who the Jews and other Semitic peoples believed responsible for all events. But whatever the beliefs, whether monotheistic or polytheistic, worshippers everywhere created symbols to characterize themselves and their groups and to express their beliefs.

Latin Cross
Tau Cross
St. Peter's Cross
Thieves' Cross
Cross of Lorraine
Papal Cross
Russian Cross
St. Andrew's Cross
Greek Cross
Maltese Cross
Celtic Cross
Egyptian Cross

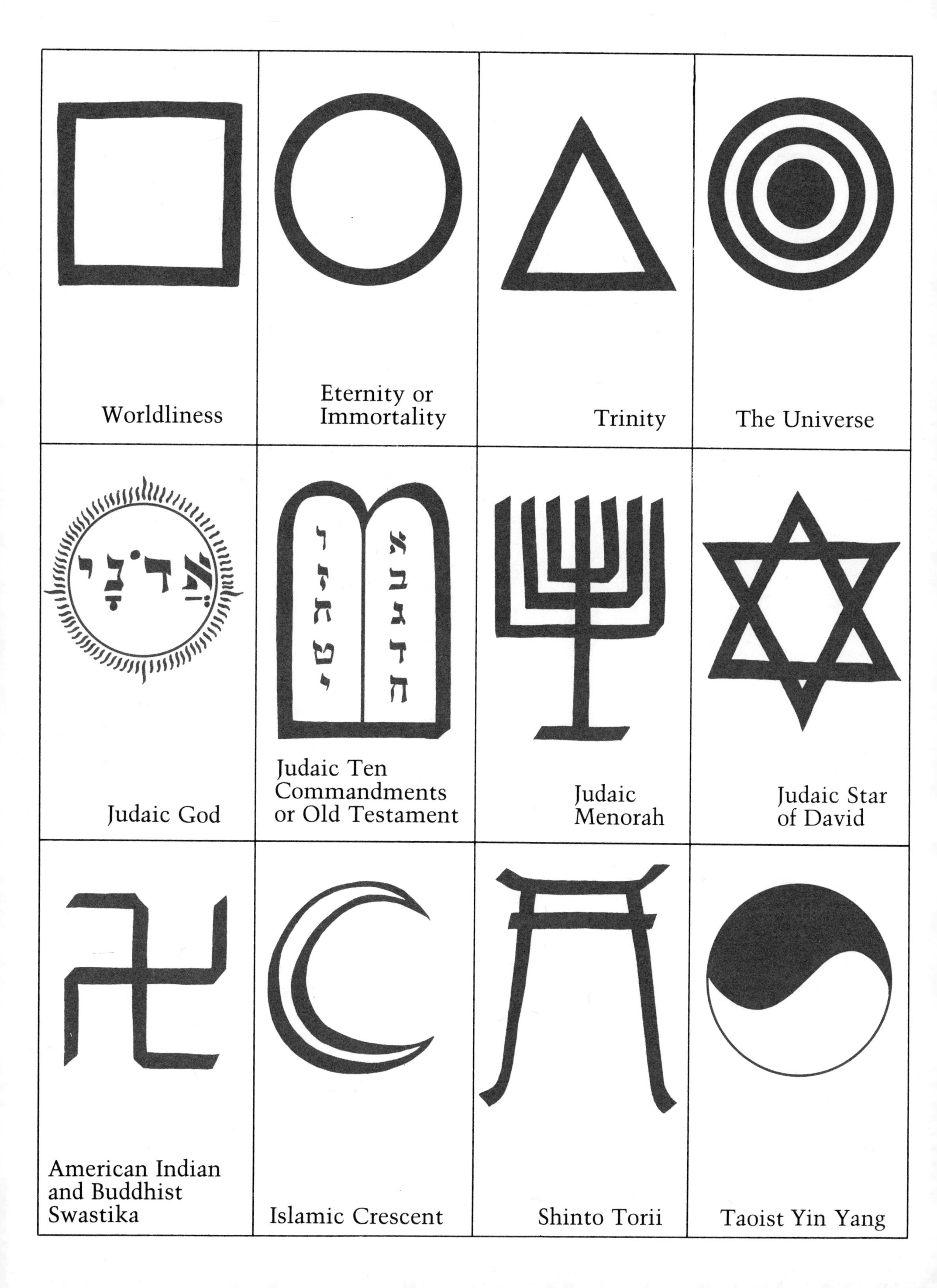
Worldliness
Eternity or Immortality
Trinity
The Universe
Judaic God
Judaic Ten Commandments or Old Testament
Judaic Menorah
Judaic Star of David
American Indian and Buddhist Swastika
Islamic Crescent
Shinto Torii
Taoist Yin Yang

SYMBOL
ART

SHORTHAND

The command "Take a letter" is a familiar one to a *stenographer*—someone who writes in shorthand. To take a letter, the stenographer writes the words being dictated on a pad of paper. The writing, in all likelihood, is not the words in the letters we recognize, but a different series of symbols expressing the sounds of the words. Later, the shorthand symbols are converted on a typewriter or word processor to the words in our twenty-six-letter alphabet.

Modern shorthand systems of writing began in England in 1837 when Isaac Pitman published *Stenographic Sound-Hand,* a book devoted to the Pitman shorthand method. Actually, shorthand writing was nothing new. The Romans used it. The Phoenicians had a shorthand system before the Romans. And there were shorthand systems during the early Middle Ages. They had all but disappeared until the Pitman system revived the useful practice a thousand years later. Pitman shorthand relied on light-stroke and dark-stroke symbols to express sound. And the meaning of Pitman's symbols changed, depending on where they appeared—over a line, below a line or through a line.

Fifty-one years later, in 1888, Irish-born John R. Gregg introduced a more efficient shorthand system in his book *Light-Line Phonography.* The Gregg system relied on rhythmical strokes that seemed to flow one into the other. Moreover, some of Gregg's strokes symbolized whole phrases in addition to sounds. The Gregg system was more readily adaptable to languages other than English. It soon became the most widely used shorthand system in the world.

In 1935, Charles A. Thomas, an American, invented the Thomas Natural shorthand system. Thomas tried to simplify all shorthand writing with a twelve-symbol method. But the Thomas system never succeeded in replacing the more popular Gregg or its older rival, Pitman. Strokes from the Gregg system are illustrated on the following pages.

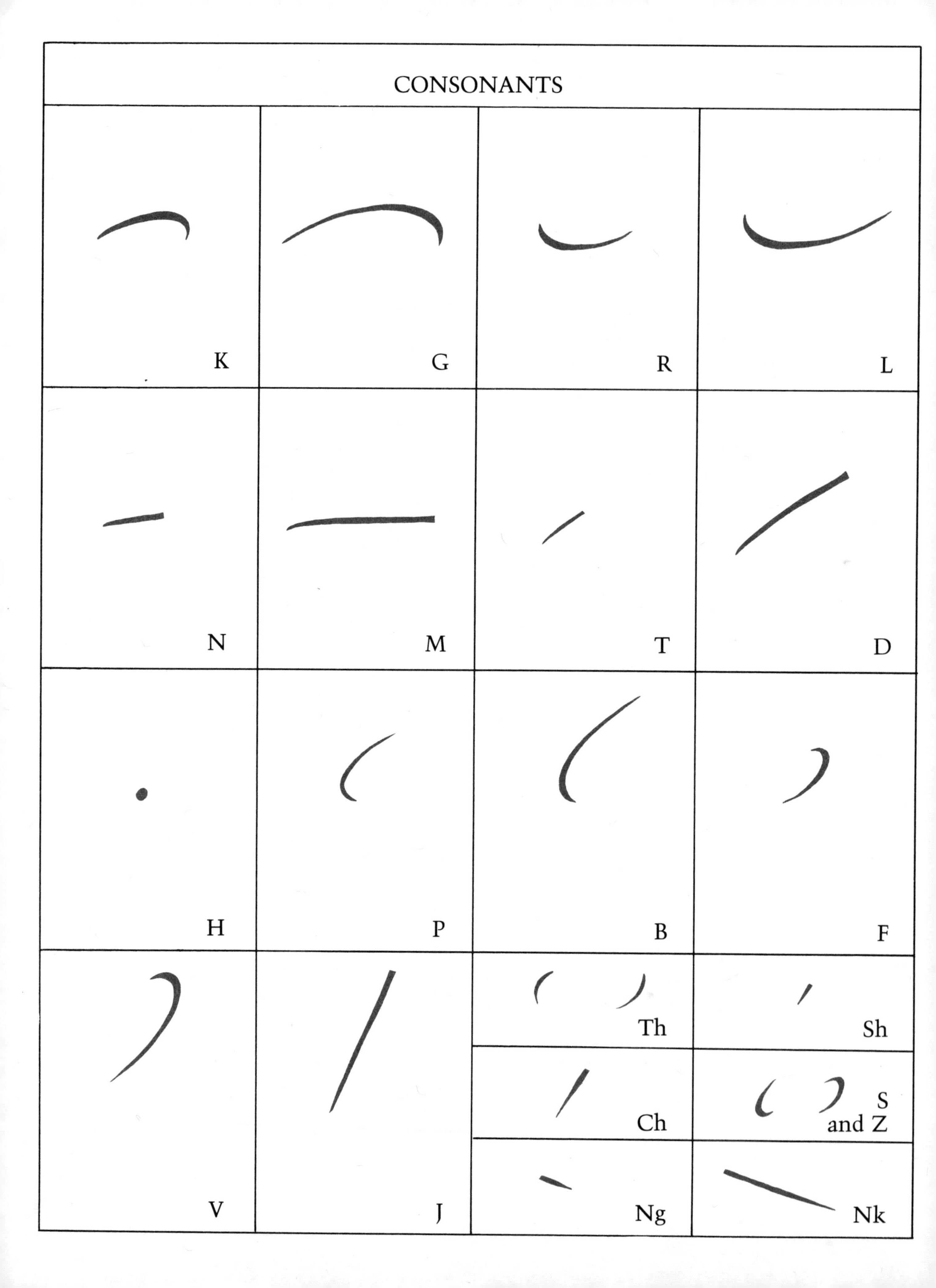
CONSONANTS
K
G
R
L
N
M
T
D
H
P
B
F
V
J
Th
Sh
Ch
S and Z
Ng
Nk

VOWELS	DIPHTHONGS	PUNCTUATION	
a *(b<u>a</u>t h<u>a</u>rm p<u>a</u>in)*	u *(chew)*	Period	Question Mark
i *(p<u>i</u>t p<u>e</u>n sh<u>ee</u>t)*	ow *(now)*	Dash	Hyphen
o *(p<u>o</u>t p<u>o</u>ke th<u>a</u>w)*	oi *(spoil)*	Paragraph	Parenthesis
u *(l<u>u</u>ck sh<u>oo</u>k sch<u>oo</u>l)*	i *(fly)*	Frequently used words and phrases that have distinctive symbol strokes of their own have not been included here. *Examples:* The, But, With, At the, In the, Nevertheless	

LEF

WEATHER

The use of symbols to forecast and record weather developed as the communication of weather information entered the mainstream of modern life toward the end of the nineteenth century.

The telegraph was invented by an American artist, Samuel Finley Breese Morse, in 1844. It provided a method—the only one at the time—to warn of coming storms or to exchange weather information. The French were the first to use Morse's telegraph to gather weather information, from all over France, and collect the reports in a central place. They used the material to predict weather patterns for farmers. France had a weather forecasting office by the 1850s. A network of weather observation posts was being established in the United States, relaying weather information over new and far-flung telegraph wires, but there was no centrally organized weather service in the United States until 1870.

In 1870, during the administration of President Ulysses S. Grant, the United States Congress ordered the Army Signal Corps to establish a national weather service. Twenty years later, in 1890, that weather service was transferred from military to civilian management in the Department of Agriculture and renamed the United States Weather Bureau. In 1940, the Weather Bureau was made part of the Department of Commerce. Today, the National Weather Service is an arm of the National Oceanic and Atmospheric Administration of the Department of Commerce. Weather information from all over the United States is gathered at the Weather Service's National Meteorological Center in Maryland. There it is analyzed, symbolized and made public by television, radio and newspapers.

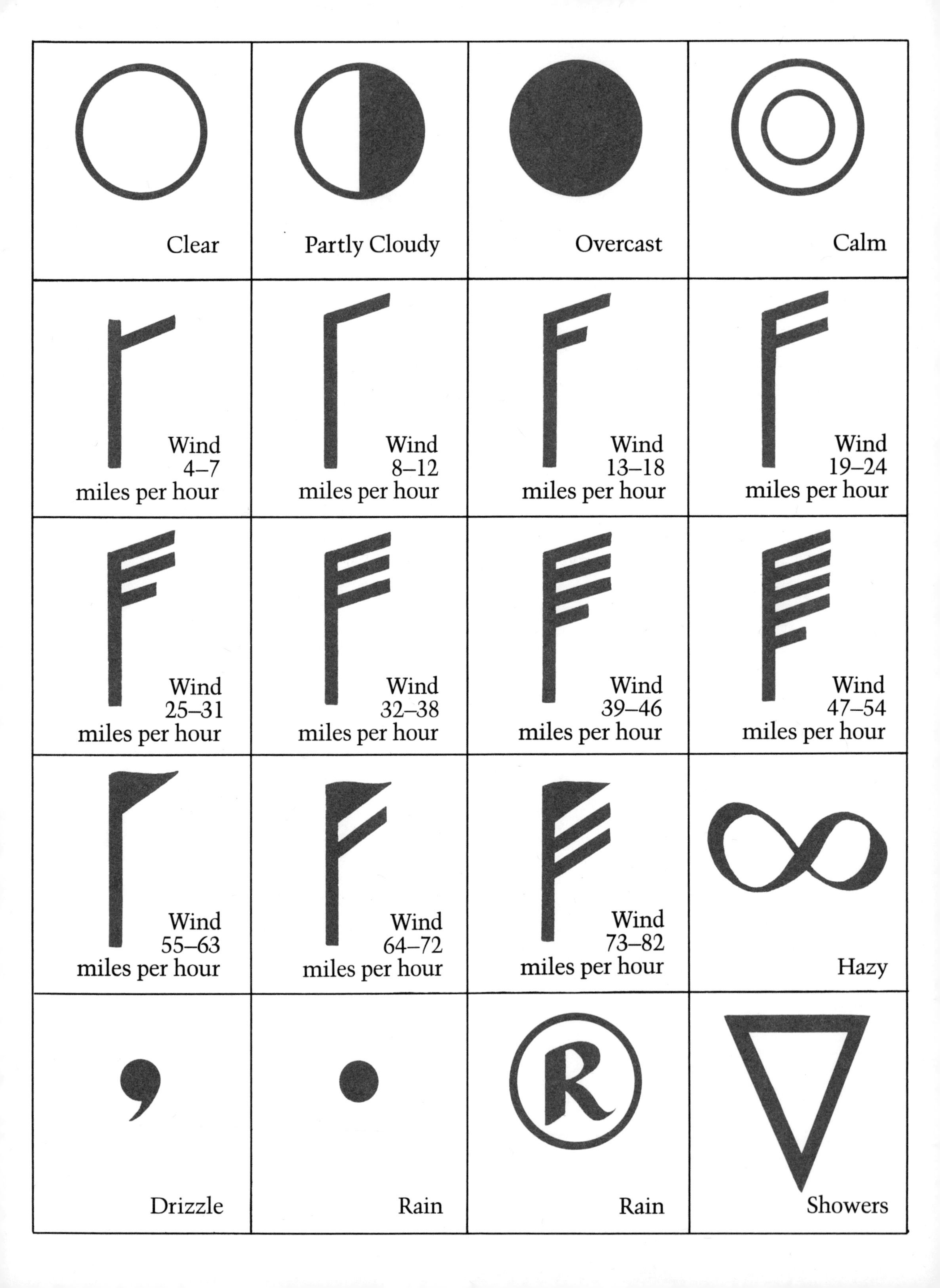
Clear
Partly Cloudy
Overcast
Calm
Wind 4–7 miles per hour
Wind 8–12 miles per hour
Wind 13–18 miles per hour
Wind 19–24 miles per hour
Wind 25–31 miles per hour
Wind 32–38 miles per hour
Wind 39–46 miles per hour
Wind 47–54 miles per hour
Wind 55–63 miles per hour
Wind 64–72 miles per hour
Wind 73–82 miles per hour
Hazy
Drizzle
Rain
Rain
Showers

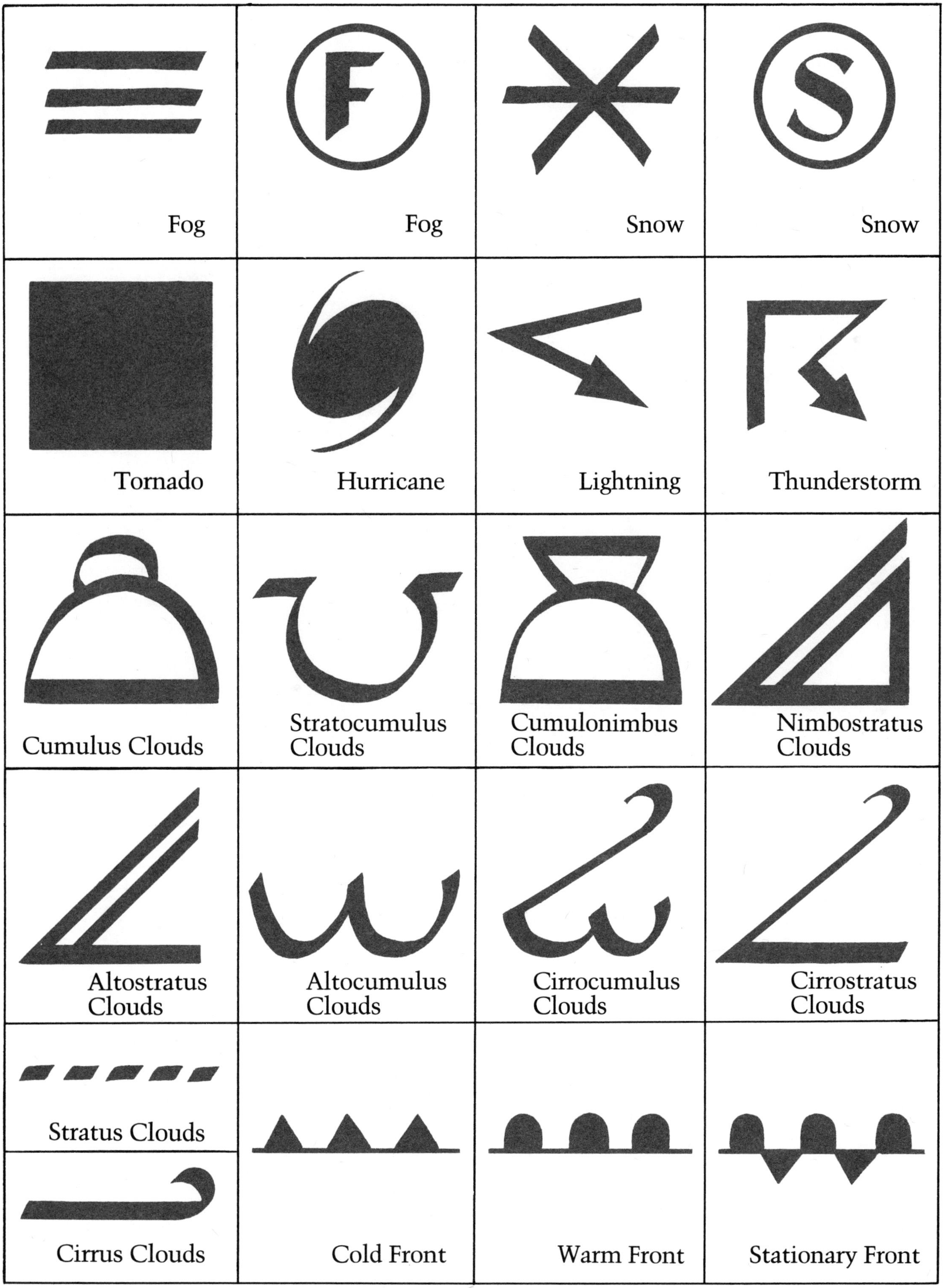

Fog

Fog

Snow

Snow

Tornado

Hurricane

Lightning

Thunderstorm

Cumulus Clouds

Stratocumulus Clouds

Cumulonimbus Clouds

Nimbostratus Clouds

Altostratus Clouds

Altocumulus Clouds

Cirrocumulus Clouds

Cirrostratus Clouds

Stratus Clouds

Cirrus Clouds

Cold Front

Warm Front

Stationary Front

upper left, Proofreader's Period; *upper right,* Egyptian Long Life; *lower left,* Sulfur; *lower right,* Per Unit